DISNEP · PIXAR

FINDING NEMO

The Tank Gang

ADVANCE PUBLISHERS

Nemo had been dared by his new friends to swim and touch a diver's boat. He wasn't supposed to go out into that part of the open ocean. After touching the boat, the little clownfish was captured by a diver!

A while later, Nemo was dropped into unfamiliar waters.
He saw a volcano and came face-to-face with strange and scary
tiki heads. As he swam, he kept bumping into invisible walls. He
didn't understand that he was in a fish tank in a dentist's office.

Center stage in Dr. Philip Sherman's dental office is the kookiest fish tank in town. This dentist has no kids to spend his money on, so he lavishes it on his favorite fish. Tiki idol heads, a working volcano, a treasure chest, a sinister skull— the gang of fish in this tank swim in a world full of myth and mystery.

Suddenly, he heard voices behind him. But when he turned around, no one was there. Nemo was very confused and very frightened.

Slowly, several fish swam out from behind the plants. Bloat, Bubbles, Peach, Jacques, Deb, and Gurgle introduced themselves to Nemo. Nigel the pelican also arrived at the window to say hello. They were all excited to meet a fish from the open sea.

Just then, the dentist, Dr. Sherman, came over. He picked up a framed picture. "This here's Darla," the dentist said to Nemo. "Going to be eight this week, and you're her present."

Ever thought how dull it would be to be stuck in a fish tank all day? Well, think again. Being part of this kooky crowd makes captivity almost seem fun. But the one thing that keeps them all going is the hope of escape. Well, that and placing bets on how many fillings each patient is going to need!

"I can't go with that girl!" Nemo cried to the other fish. He had to get home to his father.

Scared, Nemo backed up and was sucked into the tank's filter! The other fish rushed to help him, but then a voice said, "Nobody touch him."

The voice belonged to Gill, the leader of the Tank Gang.

Gill coached Nemo on how to free himself, but Nemo said, "I can't. I have a bad fin."

"Never stopped me," Gill replied, turning to show his own injured fin.

So Nemo tried again, and this time, he wiggled free.

"Fish aren't meant to be in a box, kid . . . it does things to you!" Gill tells Nemo. That sums up the attitude of this fish who always has an escape plan at the ready. Gill knows no fear. He is confident that, "all drains lead to the ocean."

That night, Jacques woke up Nemo. He led Nemo to the top of the fake volcano where the other tank fish were waiting.

"Nemo, newcomer of orange and white," began Bloat. "You have been called forth to the summit of Mount Wannahockaloogie to join with us in the fraternal bonds of tankhood."

Nemo looked confused, so Peach explained. "We want you in our club, kid."

Bloat loves hosting the mystical Ring of Fire ceremony at Mount Wannahockaloogie. He enjoys scaring the newcomer with his loud cries of "Ooh-ha-hah!" He likes being in a gang and puffs up with pride when Gill calls him Brother Bloat.

"If you are able to swim through the Ring of Fire," added Bloat.

The Ring of Fire was really just a wall of bubbles. Nemo swam through it with ease. Now, he was one of the gang!

Then Gill shared his plan for how they would all escape from the tank: First, they had to break the filter. The dentist would have to remove the fish in order to clean the tank. He'd place them in plastic bags full of water. That's when the fish would roll themselves out the window to freedom.

Nemo needed to swim into the filter and jam it with a pebble. "Let's do it!" Nemo exclaimed. He wanted to escape so he could find his father, and especially so he wouldn't be Darla's present!

It was on one of these outings that Gill and his mates were captured and ended up in a pet store. One by one, his friends accepted their fate. But Gill refused to be tamed and believes that, like Nemo, he can get back his freedom by returning to the ocean, his home, and his family.

In a few days, the fish were celebrating. Without a working filter, the water in the tank was a yucky, slimy green.

"Filthy, absolutely filthy," Gill said proudly to Nemo. "And it's all thanks to you, kid. You made it possible."

Nemo giggled and then hid as Dr. Sherman walked over to the aquarium.

It's tough on Jacques when Gill says it's time to let the tank get scummy. Although it's part of an escape plan, the shrimp can't help but want to clean. After he is told off, he allows the plan to take place while he hangs his eyes in shame.

The dentist wiped his finger across the glass. "Crikey!" he said. He decided to clean the tank the next morning before Darla arrived.

The following morning, the Tank Gang awoke to a horrible discovery. The tank had already been cleaned! The fish looked up and saw a new high-tech filter called the Aqua Scum 2020.

"Boss must have installed it last night when we were sleeping," said Gill.

"The escape plan is ruined!" wailed Bloat. At that moment, the dentist walked into the office. He put a small net into the tank , scooped up Nemo, and placed him inside a plastic bag.

Nemo and his friends were worried. Darla would be arriving any minute to take Nemo away!

Dr. Sherman takes his hobby so seriously that he cancels an appointment just to clean out his tank. He outfits it with the Aqua Scum filter. This miracle of cutting edge aquarium technology ensures that the tank will never be scummy again! It sucks away slime, and purifies salt water.

Darla gets a free check-up and a present from her uncle on her birthday. She loves fish and always shakes the bag when she gets one. Sadly, they don't last very long—like poor Chuckles, her goldfish gift from last year. The Tank Gang live in terror of Darla's visits as she likes to scream at the fish and thump the tank to liven them up.

"Fishy, fishy, fishy!" Darla cried as she came into the room.

The dentist reached for the bag. Inside, Nemo was floating upside down—he was playing dead! The Tank Gang cheered. If the dentist flushed Nemo down the toilet, he'd travel down the drain and end up in the ocean.

But they watched with horror as Dr. Sherman started walking over to the trash can instead!

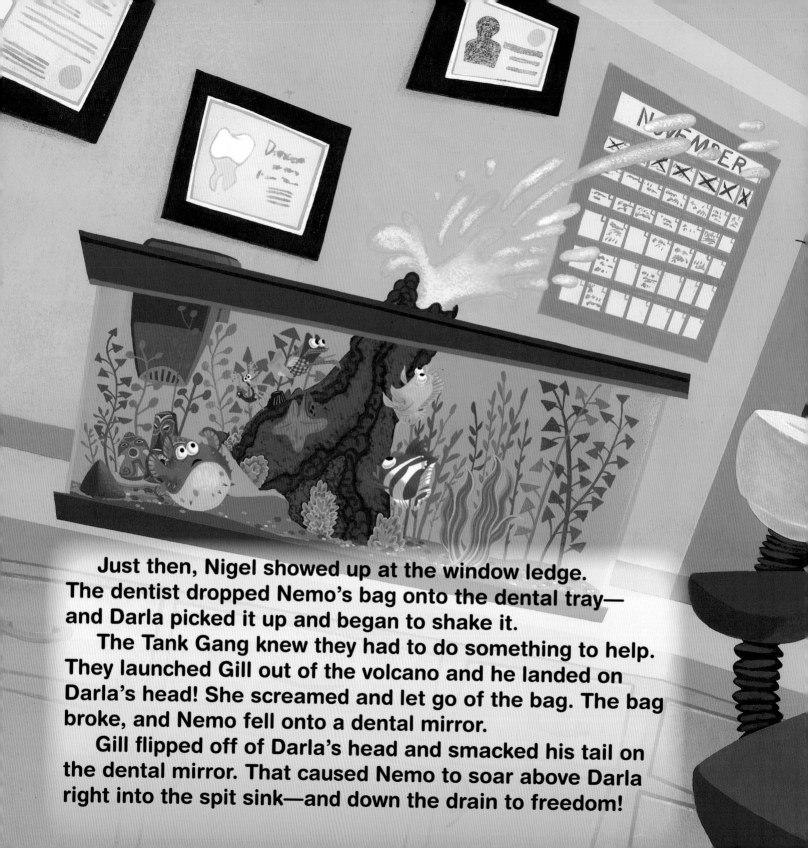

Just then, Nigel showed up at the window ledge. The dentist dropped Nemo's bag onto the dental tray— and Darla picked it up and began to shake it.

The Tank Gang knew they had to do something to help. They launched Gill out of the volcano and he landed on Darla's head! She screamed and let go of the bag. The bag broke, and Nemo fell onto a dental mirror.

Gill flipped off of Darla's head and smacked his tail on the dental mirror. That caused Nemo to soar above Darla right into the spit sink—and down the drain to freedom!

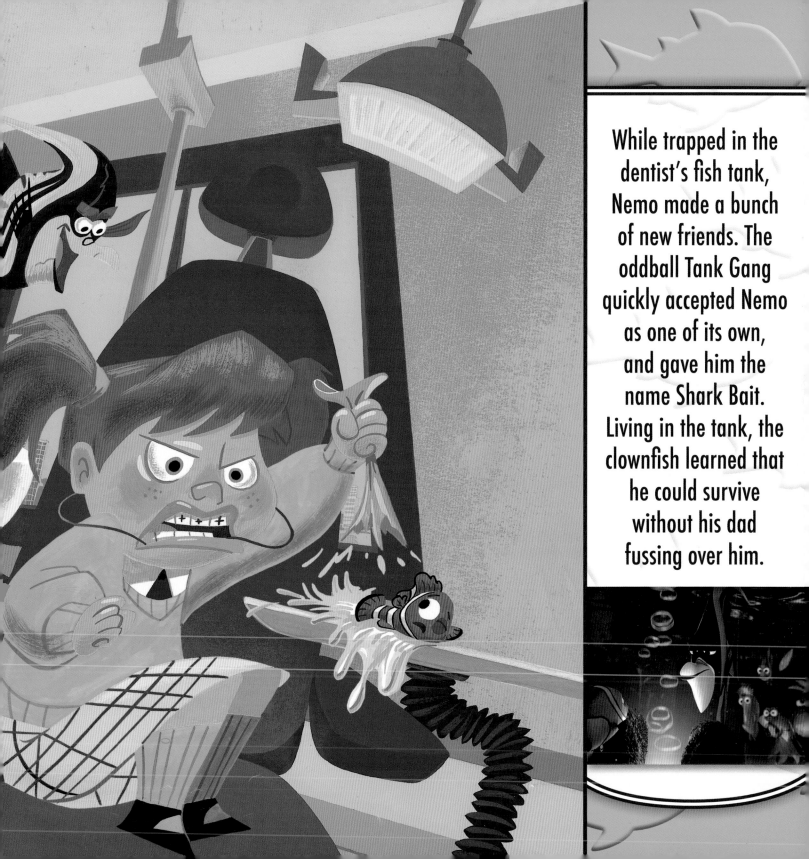

While trapped in the dentist's fish tank, Nemo made a bunch of new friends. The oddball Tank Gang quickly accepted Nemo as one of its own, and gave him the name Shark Bait. Living in the tank, the clownfish learned that he could survive without his dad fussing over him.

In the ocean, Nemo finally found his father.
"Love ya, Dad," said Nemo.
"I love you too, son," said his father.

Meanwhile, the tank fish had finally made their daring escape. They had managed to break the Aqua Scum 2020, forcing the dentist to clean the tank.

Now they just had to figure out how to get out of those bags!

Sydney Harbour teems with fishing boats, ferries, cruise ships, and sailing boats. Overlooking the harbour is Sydney Harbour Bridge, known to locals as the Coat Hanger. Dr. Sherman's boat, the *Aussie Flosser*, is anchored somewhere in the harbour.

JOKES, RIDDLES, AND SILLY STUFF!

Still hungry for volume 1 answers?

What's gray and wears a crown?
The Prince of Whales.

Where do fish go on Halloween?
Lake Eerie.

What lives in the ocean, has tentacles, and is quick on the draw?
Billy The Squid.

What do whales like to chew?
Blubber gum.

What sits under the ocean and shakes?
A nervous wreck.

Did Bruce the Shark have a good vacation?
Yes, it was very en-jaw-able!

What do baby sharks love to eat?
Peanut butter and jellyfish sandwiches.

What is the worst day of the week for fish?
Fry-day.

How do you make a jellyfish laugh?
Give him ten tickles!

What is Bruce's favorite ice cream?
Sharkolate.

How does an octopus go into battle?
Well-armed.

What says "How do you do?" 16 times?
Two octopuses shaking hands.

What did Pearl, the Octopus, get for her birthday?
Four pairs of gloves.

What do you get when you cross fish with elephants?
Swimming trunks.

What's gray, likes fish and lives in Washington, D.C.?
The Presidential Seal.

Which was the first fish in space?
A starfish.

What's yellow and fuzzy and lies on the beach?
A peach blanket.

What's yellow and fuzzy and rides on the beach?
A peach buggy.

Why do seagulls fly south?
Because it's too far to walk.

What do you call a seagull that flies over the bay?
A bay-gull. (A bagel!)

What do fishing poles want?
A reel family.

How did the dentist cross the river?
On a tooth ferry.

What's a pelican become after it is four days old?
Five days old.

What's the most famous fish?
A starfish.

What do sharks eat?
Fish and ships.

What time is it when a whale hits your boat?
Time to get a new boat.

What whale can fly?
A pilot whale.

Which whales are sad?
Blue whales.